Throwing sponges at Principal!

First, I got the sponge from under the sink. Then I made it soaky wet with water.

I pointed it at the target.

"Ready...aim...fire!" I said.

Then I throwed the sponge with all my might.

It splashed right in the middle of the toilet pot!

"BULL'S-EYE! I MADE A BULL'S-EYE!" I hollered real excited.

But just then, I heard a knock at the door.

It was Mother!

"OPEN UP RIGHT NOW, YOUNG LADY!" she yelled.

The Junie B. Jones series by Barbara Park

Junie B. Jones and the Stupid Smelly Bus #1
Junie B. Jones and a Little Monkey Business #2
Junie B. Jones and Her Big Fat Mouth #3
Junie B. Jones and Some Sneaky Peeky Spying #4
Junie B. Jones and the Yucky Blucky Fruitcake #5

Junie B. Jones
and the
Yucky Blucky Fruitcake

by Barbara Park

illustrated by Denise Brunkus

SCHOLASTIC INC.

New York Toronto London Auckland Sydney
Mexico City New Delhi Hong Kong

ISBN 0-439-13502-8

72 71 70 69 68   14 15 16/0

Printed in the U.S.A.   40

First Scholastic printing, November 1999

Contents

1/
The Bestest
Game Winner

My name is Junie B. Jones. The B stands for Beatrice. Except I don't like Beatrice. I just like B and that's all.

I am in the grade of kindergarten. It is the afternoon kind.

Afternoon kindergarten is better than morning kindergarten. That's because you get to sleep late. And watch cartoons.

Only guess what? Today my baby brother named Ollie waked me up very too early.

He was screaming for his bottle.

But screaming is not polite. And so he needed some discipline, I think.

I sat up in my bed.

"HEY! SHUT UP YOUR FACE!" I hollered.

Mother opened my door speedy quick.

Her eyes were angry at me.

"Junie B. Jones! What do you think you're doing?" she growled.

I hided from her under my sheet.

"I think I'm doin' discipline," I said kind of quiet.

"*Please*, Junie B. *Not* today," said Mother. "Daddy and I need you to be on your best behavior. We both have to go to work early and Grampa Miller is coming to baby-sit."

Just then, I heard the front door open.

"GRAMPA! IT'S MY GRAMPA

FRANK MILLER!" I shouted.

I jumped out of bed and ran to meet him. Only too bad for Grampa. 'Cause he didn't see me coming around the corner. And I accidentally butted him in the stomach with my head.

Grampa Miller yelled the word of *OOOMF!*

Then he bended way over in half. And me and Mother and Daddy had to help him walk to the couch.

Daddy did a frown at me.

"How many times have we told you not to run in the house?" he said.

I counted on all my fingers. "A million thrillion skadillion, I think. Only I'm just guessing."

After that, Mother made me sit on her lap. And she told Grampa Frank Miller the baby-sitter 'structions on me.

Baby-sitter 'structions is all the stuff I'm not allowed to do.

Like no climbing on top of the 'frigerator.

And no putting lipstick on my dog named Tickle.

And no making Ollie lick a potato. Except for he didn't actually mind it that much.

After the baby-sitter 'structions, Mother and Daddy kissed me good-bye.

Then they went to work.

I jumped way high in the air.

"Oh boy! Oh boy! Now they're gone! And so you and me can have fun! Right, Grampa? Right?"

I zoomed into the kitchen and climbed on top of the 'frigerator.

"HEY, GRAMPA! COME LOOK WHERE I AM!"

4

Grampa Miller came in the kitchen.
"Look! Look how high I am up here!
Now I can be the king. And this can be my

throne. And you're my servant named Pinkie. And you have to fetch me stuff. And also I get to hit you on the head with my sword."

Grampa Miller lifted me off the 'frigerator. He put me back on the floor.

"Yeah, only I didn't give you permission to do that, Pinkie," I said.

"Sorry, little girl. But you heard the rules," said Grampa. "And anyhow, I have to finish feeding Ollie his breakfast bottle."

He went back into the living room.

"Hey, Grampa! You just gave me a very great idea! 'Cause I think I'll eat *my* breakfast, too. Only I can fix mine all by myself!"

I hurried up and got out the 'greedients. 'Greedients is the stuff you mix together.

Like the bowl.

And the spoon.

And the cereal.

And the milk.

Except for the milk carton was very too heavy for me. And so I just got the orange juice, instead.

I put my bowl of cereal on the floor. Then I poured orange juice to the tippy-top of it.

I took a giant bite.

"Yum," I said. "This is the most delicious breakfast I ever ate. Except for it doesn't actually taste that good."

Just then Grampa Miller came in the kitchen. He said no eating on the floor.

"Yeah, but I don't like to sit in my big kitchen chair," I said. "'Cause I'm not tall enough to reach the table. And so Mother makes me sit on a telephone book. Only that thing hurts my behiney."

My grampa looked in my bowl. "What in the world are you eating?" he asked.

"I am eating cereal and orange juice," I told him. "It is very delicious. Except for it is going to make me puke, I think."

Then Grampa Frank Miller opened the 'frigerator. So he could find me a better kind of breakfast.

"How 'bout some fruit?" he said.

"Yea!" I shouted. "Yea for fruit! 'Cause fruit is the bestest thing I love!"

I folded my hands very polite. "I would like some bananas and some peaches and some strawberries, please!"

And so Grampa sliced all those fruits into a bowl. And he let me eat them in the living room. In front of TV!

And I'm not even allowed to do that! Only we're not telling Mother!

And here's another fun thing!

After breakfast, baby Ollie took his nap. And me and my grampa Miller played Old

Maid. And I winned him five whole times in a row!

That's because I kept on putting the old maid way higher than the rest of my cards. And he kept on picking it!

Grampa Frank Miller is a sucker, I think.

Me and him played lots more games, too.

Their names are Who Can Skip the Fastest. And Who Can Hop on One Foot the Longest. And also the game of Tic-Tac-Toad.

And guess what? I winned all of those games, too!

"I'm the bestest game winner in the whole world!" I said.

Then I runned to my room to get ready for kindergarten.

First, I put on my favorite pants with the polka dotties on them.

Then, I found my favorite sweater with

the cow on the front. It was in the dirty clothes hamper. Only it didn't even stink that much.

After that, I combed my hair with my fingers. And I brushed my teeth. Except for not the wiggly one.

Grampa made me a sandwich for lunch. Its name was Jack Cheese.

I ate it all up. Then I gave him a big kiss. And I skipped to my school bus very happy.

"I'M THE BESTEST WINNN-ERRRR. I'M THE BESTEST WINNN-ERRRR," I sang real loud.

'Cause winning is the funnest thing I love.

2
Hopping and Racing and Tic-Tac-Toad

I ride the school bus with my bestest friend named Grace.

She has curly black hair. That is my favorite kind of head.

Also she has pink high tops with big feet in them.

That Grace is a lucky duck, I think.

"Hey, Grace! Guess what? Me and my grampa Frank Miller played games today! And I winned him at Old Maid and at hopping and skipping and Tic-Tac-Toad!

11

And so I am the bestest game winner in the whole world!"

That Grace smiled. "Me, too," she said. "I'm a good game winner, too."

I patted her very nice. "Yeah, only you can't be as good as me, Grace. 'Cause I said it first, that's why."

That Grace did a mad face at me. Then she called me the name of beanie head.

I patted her again.

"You don't take criticism that well, Grace," I said.

Just then she got out a pencil and paper from her back pack.

She drew a Tic-Tac-Toad.

"Now we'll see who the bestest winner *really* is," she said.

"I GOT X's!" I hollered.

"I GOT O's!" she hollered.

"I GO FIRST!" I hollered.

"I GO SECOND!" she hollered.

Then me and her played Tic-Tac-Toad.

"TIC-TAC-TOAD! THREE IN A ROAD!" I yelled very fast. "SEE, GRACE? SEE? I TOLD YA I'M THE BESTEST WINNER!"

That Grace looked at the paper.

"But your X's aren't in a *row*, Junie B.," she said.

I did a huffy breath at her.

"I *know* they are not in a row, Grace. That is why I made a curvy line to connect them."

That Grace jumped up.

"Cheater! Cheater! That's cheating!" she shouted. "The X's have to be in a straight row!"

Then she passed our Tic-Tac-Toad all around the bus. And all the other kids called me cheater too.

Plus a mean boy named Jim called me the name of nutball.

I hate that guy.

After that, I scooted way over next to the window all by myself.

"I shoulda took O's," I whispered very disappointed.

Pretty soon, the bus pulled into my school parking lot.

I hurried off that thing speedy quick.

"Hey, Junie B.! Wait up!" yelled that Grace. "You and me can skip to the swing set together. Want to?"

And so all of a sudden, I felt happy inside again. 'Cause skipping is my bestest game! I could cream her at that, I think!

"Hey, Grace!" I hollered. "You and me can have a skipping race! The first one to the swings is the winner!"

I took a big breath.

"READY…GET SET…GO!" I shouted.

Except for that Grace wasn't actually off the bus yet.

Only that's not my problem.

I skipped as fast as a speeding rocket.

"I'm winning! I'm winning!" I shouted very thrilled.

But just then, that Grace skipped right past me.

"Hi, Junie B.…bye, Junie B.!" she said.

Then she touched the swing set before I did.

"I won! I won!" she yelled. "I beat you at skipping! I *told* you I was a good game winner!"

I stamped my foot at her. "No, you are not a good game winner, Grace," I said. "'Cause your feet are way gianter than mine. And also you have pink high tops. So this race was not fair and square."

That Grace stuck her tongue out at me.

"That is not attractive of you, madam," I said.

Then I turned around and saw my other bestest friend named Lucille!

I runned to her speedy quick.

"Hey, Lucille! It's me! It's your bestest friend, Junie B. Jones! Let's not play with that Grace, okay? Let's just play by ourselves. 'Cause you and me can have a hopping contest! And we can see who's the bestest hopper!"

Lucille fluffed her lacy dress.

"Okay, but I'm not allowed to get sweaty. And also I must be careful of my fingernails."

She showed them to me.

"See? The manicure lady painted them Apricot Ice. See how beauteous they are?"

"Yeah, yeah, whatever," I said not looking.

I took a giant breath.

"READY…GET SET…GO!" I shouted.

Then me and Lucille started hopping on one foot.

We hopped and hopped and hopped.

Only it wasn't as fun as hopping with Grampa Miller. On account of Lucille didn't get tired and fall over.

"Look, Junie B.!" she said very squealy. "Look how bouncy I am! This is fun! Isn't it?"

I wiped my sweating head.

"Yeah, only it would be funner if you fell over now, Lucille. 'Cause I just had a skipping contest with that Grace. And I'm a little pooped here."

"Look, Junie B.!" she said again. "Look

how my fluffy skirt bounces over my head when I hop way high!"

My face felt hottish and reddish.

"I can see your underpants, Lucille," I told her.

Only that dumb Lucille didn't even care if I could see her underpants. She just kept on hopping and hopping.

Finally, I got tired and fell over.

"Yea! Yea!" shouted Lucille. "I'm the

winner! I'm the winner of hopping!"

Just then, the school bell rang. And everybody ran to Room Nine.

Except for not me.

I walked very slow.

All by myself.

Mrs. was standing outside Room Nine.

Mrs. is the name of my teacher. She has another name, too. But I just like Mrs. and that's all.

She smiled at me.

"Why so glum today, Junie B.?" she asked.

"'Cause people keep on beating me at all my games, that's why. And so now I'm not the bestest winner anymore," I said.

Then I went to my seat. And I put my head down on my table.

On account of glum is when the happy is gone right out of you.

3/ All About Carnivals

Mrs. took attendance.

Attendance is when you say the word *here*. Only I didn't feel like saying it. So I just raised my hand very flimsy.

"Are you feeling all right, Junie B.?" Mrs. asked.

"She's okay," said Lucille. "She's just mad because I beat her at hopping."

"YEAH, ONLY I ALREADY EX-PLAINED THAT TO YOU, MADAM!" I shouted at Lucille's face.

Mrs. clapped her loud hands at me.

"Junie B. Jones! That will be enough of that!" she said.

I put my head on my table again. "This day is a bummer," I whispered to just myself.

Mrs. stood up at her desk.

"Boys and girls. May I have your attention, please? I would like to talk to you about a special night coming up at school on Friday. It's called Carnival Night. Does anyone know what a carnival is?"

"I do! I do!" said that Jim I hate. "A carnival is like what they have at the state fair every year. There're lots of rides there. Like the Ferris wheel and the Tilt-A-Whirl and the bumper cars."

"Yeah, and there's a shooting gallery with fake ducks," said Jamal Hall.

"And there's cotton candy that rots your teeth by eating big black holes in your

21

protective tooth enamel," said a boy I love named Ricardo.

Ricardo's mother is a dentist, I think.

After that, a crybaby boy named William stood up very shy. And he said one time he rode the scary roller coaster. And he didn't even cry that much. Except for he accidentally threw up his chili dog.

Then Paulie Allen Puffer told about carnival food that he threw up, too.

Like a candy apple.

And caramel popcorn.

And a rubber band.

Except for that is not food. That is office supplies.

I raised my hand. "Carnivals are rip-offs," I said. "'Cause one time my daddy kept on trying to knock over three bottles with a ball. But even when he hit them, they wouldn't fall down. So then he and Mother had to call the cops. And also Eyewitness News at Six and Ten."

Mrs. laughed out loud.

"Yeah, only that is not a laughing matter," I told her.

She stopped smiling.

"No. Of course it isn't," she said. "But I promise that nothing like that will happen at our school's Carnival Night, Junie B. All the games are going to be run by the parents and teachers. And there will be hundreds of prizes to win."

I sat up a little bit straighter.

"Hundreds?" I said.

"Hundreds," she said.

"Yeah, only I don't even know how to win them," I said.

And so Mrs. got out a piece of paper that

told all about the carnival games.

"Well, let's see," she said. "It says there will be a Fishing Booth, a Penny Toss, a Moon Walk Tent, a Putting Green, Clothespins in the Bottle, a Basketball Shoot, a Ring Toss, and a booth where you can throw wet sponges at our principal's face."

Just then Room Nine started laughing very much. 'Cause throwing sponges at Principal is a dream come true, that's why.

Mrs. kept on reading. "It also says that Mrs. Hall, the art teacher, will be painting faces in the art room. And in our very own Room Nine, there is going to be a Cake Walk."

I jumped right out of my chair.

"Hey! Guess what? Walking on cake is the funnest thing I love! 'Cause one time at a picnic, I stepped on my grampa's Little Debbie snack cake with bare feet. And the

24

creamy filling was very squishing between my toes!"

"GOONIE!" shouted out that Jim I hate. "YOU GOONIE BIRD JONES! YOU DON'T *WALK* ON CAKE! A CAKE WALK IS A GAME WHERE YOU *WIN* A CAKE! RIGHT, TEACHER? RIGHT?"

Mrs. made squinting eyes at him.

"Yes, Jim. But we do not call people goonie birds. Calling people names is rude. Plus—if you want to make a comment—I would appreciate it if you would politely raise your hand."

"LIKE ME! RIGHT, MRS.?" I hollered out. "'CAUSE I RAISED MY HAND VERY POLITE WHEN I TOLD YOU THAT CARNIVALS WERE RIP-OFFS! REMEM-BER THAT?"

Then a lot of other kids shouted that they were very polite, too.

And so I had to stand up on my chair so
Mrs. could hear me.

"YEAH, ONLY THEY CAN'T BE AS
POLITE AS ME! RIGHT, MRS.? 'CAUSE

I SAID IT FIRST! RIGHT? RIGHT?"

Then Mrs. rubbed her head for a very long time.

And also she took some aspirin.

4/ Very Practicing

After school, I runned all the way home from my bus stop. That's because Grandma Miller baby-sits me in the afternoon. And I wanted to tell her all about Carnival Night!

"HEY, GRANDMA MILLER! IT'S ME! IT'S JUNIE B. JONES! YOUR GRAND-GIRL! I'VE GOT SOME IMPORTANT NEWS FOR YOU! THERE'S GONNA BE A CARNIVAL AT MY SCHOOL! AND I CAN WIN A HUNDRED PRIZES AT THAT THING!"

Grandma Miller hurried out of baby

Ollie's room. She looked grumpity at me.

"Shh! Junie B.! Not so loud! I just put the baby down for his nap!"

My shoulders got very slumping.

"Yeah, only I'm excited down here, Helen," I said.

Then Grandma smiled a little bit.

And she hugged me hello.

And she said not to call her Helen.

"Yeah, only I didn't even tell you the bestest part yet!" I said. "'Cause Mrs. read me the kind of games they're going to play. And so now I can practice them at home. And I will be the bestest game winner of anyone!"

I hurried to the laundry room to get the clothespins.

"They're gonna have a game where you drop clothespins in a bottle!" I hollered to Grandma. "Except for I can't find a bottle in this whole big laundry room. So I'm just gonna drop these clothespins in a bucket. 'Cause that will give me the feel of it, I think!"

I got the bucket away from the mop. Then I dropped all of my clothespins right in that thing.

"Hey, Grandma! I did it! I did it! I dropped every single clothespin in this big bucket. And I didn't even miss one of them! I am a breeze at this game!"

I ran back to her. "Now I need some pennies to practice the Penny Toss," I said.

And so Grandma Miller gave me all her pennies. And I ran back and threw those guys in the bucket, too!

And here's another fun thing! When Mother came home from work, she showed me how to putt with a real actual golf club!

Only *no golf balls in the house.* So I just

putted a grapefruit. And also a dinner roll.

And guess what? That night at dinner I didn't even growl about sitting on the telephone book. 'Cause everything was going my way, that's why!

After we ate, Mother and Daddy cleaned up the dishes together.

They weren't even paying attention to me.

That's how come I sneaked into the bathroom to practice another game.

Its name is Throwing Sponges at Principal!

First, I got the sponge from under the sink.

Then I made it soaky wet with water.

"Ready...

"Aim...

"Fire!" I said.

Then I throwed the sponge with all my might.

It splashed right in the middle of the toilet pot!

"BULL'S-EYE! I MADE A BULL'S-EYE!" I hollered real excited.

Only just then, I heard a knock at the door.

"Junie B.? What are you doing in there? Open the door."

Oh no!

It was Mother!

I was in big trouble, I think.

My heart got very pumping. On account of I'm not actually allowed to play in the toilet.

So I quick flushed the sponge down the pot.

Only too bad for me. 'Cause that dumb thing got stucked in the hole.

And the water kept on getting higher.

And higher.

And then it runned right over the top!

Mother banged harder.

"I SAID OPEN THE DOOR!"

I did a gulp.

"Yeah, only it's a little bit splashy in here right now," I explained kind of quiet.

Mother unlocked the door with the key.

I smiled very pleasant.

"Hello. How are you today?" I said.

Mother hollered the name of ROBERT!

Robert is my daddy. Except for sometimes he is Bob.

He came running in there.

"Well, good night, folks," I said.

Then I tried to sneak out of there. But Mother held on to my shirt. And so even when I kept on walking, I kept on staying.

She made me help her and Daddy dry up the water with towels.

After that, I had to take a bath. Only I don't know why. 'Cause I was already wet from the toilet.

After my bath, Mother tucked me into bed. Me and her had a little talk.

"Look, Junie B., Daddy and I know you're excited about the carnival," she said. "And we also know you're having fun practicing the games. But you're worrying too much about winning. Nobody can win *all* of the time.

"Right?" she said.

"Right," I said.

"And besides, the fun of a school carnival isn't whether you win or lose," she said. "The fun of a school carnival is just playing the games in the first place.

"Right?" she said.

"Right," I said.

"So we'll go to Carnival Night on Friday. And we'll have a great time. And we won't worry if we don't win any prizes at all.

"Right?" she said.

"Right," I said.

Mother kissed me goodnight. "See you in the morning," she said.

"Right," I said.

After she closed my door, I waited for her feet to walk away. Then I quick took out my flashlight from under my pillow.

I shined it all around my room.

First, I shined it on my dresser.

Then I shined it on my toy box.

Then I shined it on the brand-new book-shelf Daddy made me.

I smiled and smiled.

"*That's* where I'm going to put them," I whispered to just myself.

"That is where I'm going to put my hundred prizes."

5/ Stupid Dumb Carnival Games

Carnival Night was Friday after dinner.

Daddy drove me and Mother there in the car. Only not baby Ollie. 'Cause he is a fussbudget, that's why.

I unbuckled my seat belt and looked out the window.

"Hey!" I said. "Look at all the lights on the playground! It looks like a real alive carnival out there!"

I looked harder.

"And guess what else? There are clowns

37

at this place! Only don't let them get near of me, okay? 'Cause clowns are not normal, I think.

"HEY! THERE'S MY BESTEST FRIEND NAMED LUCILLE!" I yelled.

I hurried up out of the car.

"LUCILLE! HEY! LUCILLE! LOOK! IT'S ME! IT'S JUNIE B. JONES! I'M AT CARNIVAL NIGHT!"

Me and Lucille runned at each other.

She had red hearts painted on her face.

"Look at me, Junie B.! Look how beauteous I am!" she said. "I just got my face painted by Mrs. Hall, the art teacher!"

She puckered her lips at me.

"And see my lips? My nanna put red lipstick on them so they would match my hearts!"

Lucille's lips were shiny and slickish. I tried to touch the bottom one. But

Lucille said, "Don't smudge me."

Just then, Mother and Daddy caught up with me.

Daddy had bought tickets for all the carnival games.

"Ready to get started?" he said.

"Yes!" I said. "'Cause I've been waiting for this exciting evening my whole entire career!"

I runned and runned till I found my most favorite game. Its name was Putting the Golf Ball.

There was a long green carpet there. The carpet had a little hole with a flagpole in it. And also there was a man holding golf clubs.

I ran up to him.

"Guess what? I'm going to win a prize at this thing," I said. "'Cause I've been practicing my putting very hard."

"Good for you," said the man.

Then he gave me a golf club. And he put a teeny white ball in front of me.

It was the teeniest ball I ever saw.

I looked at it for a real long time.

Then I tapped on him.

"I mostly just putt grapefruit," I explained.

The man did a frown. "Hurry up, okay? There are other children waiting," he said.

"Yeah, only I can also use a dinner roll," I told him.

"Please!" he grouched. "Just hit the ball."

And so that's how come I felt pressure inside me. And I swinged the golf club way far back. And I hit the teeny ball very hard.

It zoomed right off the green carpet.

Then it flied in the air.

And it bounced and bounced.

And people shouted the word of *ouch*.

I quick gave the man back his golf club. Then me and Mother and Daddy rushed out of there very fast.

Mother looked upset.

"Why don't we try a game where she can't actually kill someone," she said.

"HEY! I KNOW A GAME WHERE I CAN'T ACTUALLY KILL SOMEONE!" I shouted. "AND ITS NAME IS CLOTHES-PINS IN A BOTTLE!"

I runned and runned till I found it.

"Clothespins, please!" I said to the lady.

She gave me five of them. Then she told me all the 'structions.

"Just hold the clothespins at waist level and drop them—one at a time—into this milk bottle," she said.

She put an empty milk bottle down at my feet. It had a little hole at the top where the milk pours out.

"Drop two clothespins in the bottle and you win a prize," she said.

I stared and stared at the little hole.

"How come that hole is so little do you think?" I asked the lady.

"I don't know," she said. "Just go ahead and start."

I scratched my head.

"Yeah, only I don't even know how cows can squirt their milk into such a teeny thing," I said.

The lady tapped her foot. "There are other children waiting," she told me.

I looked up at her.

"Have you ever thought about using a bucket?" I asked.

"Just go!" she grouched.

And so then I felt pressure inside me again. And I hurried to drop my clothespins into the teeny hole. Only every single one of them fell right on the floor.

My eyes got tears in them.

"See?" I said. "I *told* you that dumb hole was too little."

Just then a clown saw me being sad. And he grinned a giant smile at me.

I hided behind Mother's skirt. "Don't let him get near of me," I told her.

Only the clown runned right over. And he peeked his white face close to me.

His teeth were big and yellowish.

"BACK OFF, CLOWN!" I shouted.

Then Daddy closed his eyes. And Mother said the word *oh my.*

After that, me and Mother had a little talk. It was called—no screaming back off, clown. Only I never even heard of that rule before.

My nose got sniffly.

"Carnival Night isn't being fun," I said very sad.

And so that's how come Daddy bought me an ice cream cone. And Mother bought me a red balloon.

Only too bad for me. 'Cause when she handed me the string, my ice cream dropped on the ground. And my balloon string slipped right out of my fingers.

I bended my head back and watched my balloon float up to the sky.

Then my eyes got more tears in them.

And I said the word of *poop.*

6 / Bull's-Eye

Carnival Night was being the worstest night of my life.

That's because I kept on losing at every single game.

I lost at Penny Toss.

And I lost at Ring Toss.

And also I lost at the stupid Fishing Booth. Except all you have to do is hang a fishing pole over the table. And somebody puts a toy on your pole. Only I just got a stupid dumb comb on my pole and that's all.

"Hey! What kind of stupid dumb prize is

this?" I said. "A stupid dumb comb isn't even a toy! 'Cause I can't even play with this stupid dumb thing!"

Daddy sat me down on a bench.

Me and him had another talk. It was called—stop saying the words *stupid* and *dumb*. And also I have to appreciate my comb.

Just then, I heard a voice holler at me.

"JUNIE B. JONES! HEY! JUNIE B. JONES! I'VE BEEN LOOKING ALL OVER THE PLACE FOR YOU!"

I turned around.

It was my other bestest friend, that Grace. She was holding lots of stuff in her hands.

"Look, Junie B.! Look at all my prizes! I won a shiny plastic car, and some pretty barrettes, and a delicious red lollipop, and two rubber bugs, and an eraser that looks like a hot dog! See them? See all my good stuff?"

"Yeah? So?" I said.

That Grace did a frown at me. "How come you said *yeah so*? How come you're grouchy at me, Junie B.? And why are you just sitting here on this bench?"

I did a mad breath. "I'm appreciating my comb, that's why. Don't you know anything, Grace?"

Just then, Daddy walked me away from that Grace. And he said I better shape up, little missy, or else we're going home right now.

Mother told Daddy to calm down his blood pressure.

"We have three tickets left," she said. "Let's all take some deep breaths and start all over again. What do you think, Junie B.? Do you want to try the Sponge Throw?

That sounds like fun, doesn't it?"

Then Mother held my hand. And me and her went to find the Sponge Throw. And Daddy kept on doing deep breaths.

The Sponge Throw was right in the middle of the playground.

Principal was there.

He was standing behind a board with a big clown suit painted on the front of it. Only instead of a face, there was a round hole cut in the board. And Principal's head was sticking out of it.

His face and hair were very drippity. That's because kids kept on hitting him with sponges.

It looked like the funnest game I ever saw!

I hurried up and got in line.

Except for just then something very terrible happened. And its name is, that Jim I hate got in line right behind me.

"Boo!" he said.

"You did not scare me, Jim," I said.

"Yes, I did too."

"No, you did not."

"Yes, I did too. And anyway, you shouldn't even be in this line. 'Cause girls can't throw sponges as good as boys," he said.

"Yes, they can too!" I said. "'Cause I even practiced this game at my house. And I made a bull's-eye right in my toilet pot. So there!"

That mean Jim laughed real loud.

"P.U.! JUNIE B. JONES PLAYS IN HER TOILET!" he hollered.

And so all the other kids started laughing, too.

Just then, the sponge lady tapped on me. She handed me two soaky wet sponges.

"Your turn, sister," she said.

Only I just kept standing there and standing there. 'Cause all those meanie kids wouldn't stop laughing.

"Guess what? I don't even know if I can throw these things now. 'Cause all that laughing is ruining my self-steam," I said.

"Sorry, sis. Either throw the sponges or get out of line," the lady told me.

And so finally I took a big breath. And I aimed my sponge at Principal's baldy head. And I throwed with all my muscles.

"MISSSSED HIM! YOU MISSSSED HIM! HA-HAHA-HA-HAAAA-HAAAA," sang that Jim I hate.

That's how come my temperature boiled over.

And I quick spun around.

And I throwed my other sponge right at that meanie boy's face!

It hit him right in the kisser!

"BULL'S-EYE!" I shouted very happy.

Then I runned out of that place as fast as I could. 'Cause I was in big trouble, that's why.

"Junie B. Jones!" yelled Mother.

"Junie B. Jones!" yelled Daddy.

I runned and runned till I saw the giant Moon Walk Tent.

Then I quick climbed inside of it. And I throwed my shoes out the door. 'Cause of no shoes allowed in there.

The Moon Walk Tent is like a big puffy house. You can jump far and wide in that place.

I jumped and jumped till sweat came on my head.

"This is the funnest jumping I ever saw!" I said very springy.

Except for just then the tent lady blew her whistle.

"Time's up!" she yelled.

I peeked out the door.

Mother and Daddy were waiting for me.

They weren't smiling.

"I think I'll stay in here," I said.

Only just then, Daddy came over. And he lifted me right out the door.

I smiled very pleasant.

"Hello. How are you today?" I said.

But Daddy didn't say hello. He just carried me right back to that mean Jim.

Then he made me say a 'pology to him. And also to his mother.

"Sorry I threw a sponge at your meanie boy's face," I said.

Daddy rolled his eyes way far back in his head. He carried me back to the Moon Walk Tent again.

"Get your shoes," he said. "We're going home."

"Yeah, only I was just starting to have fun," I said. "Plus I didn't even do the Cake Walk yet. And it is in my very own Room Nine."

"I told you to get your shoes," said Daddy very grumpity.

And so I went to the shoe pile. But I could only find one shoe. And not the other one.

I tapped on the tent lady.

"Can you help me find my other shoe? See what they look like? They are shiny and black with a strap that buckles. Their name is pat-and-leather."

Then me and her and Mother and Daddy looked for my other shoe. But we couldn't find it anywhere.

"Darn it," I said. "Now my feet are ruined."

I started to cry a teeny bit.

Then Daddy smoothed my hair. And he said the word *don't worry*.

"You and Mother go on to the Cake

Walk," he said. "I'll stay here and find your other shoe."

And so then Mother holded my hand.

And me and her walked to Room Nine.

With just pat.

And no leather.

7/ Winning!!!

Room Nine looked very fun. Music was playing in that place. And children were marching in a circle.

They were stepping on big squares of paper with numbers on them.

"That's the Cake Walk," Mother explained. "You walk around in a circle until the lady stops the music. Then she pulls a number out of a hat. And if you're standing on the square with the same number, you win a cake."

Mother pointed to a table with cakes on it.

"See all the delicious cakes you have to choose from?" she said.

I looked at all the delicious cakes.

Then my mouth got very watering. And I did a little bit of drool on myself.

All of a sudden, the music stopped. And all of the children stopped, too.

The cake lady reached into a hat. She pulled out a number.

"Number five!" she said very loud.

"HEY! THAT'S ME! I'M ON FIVE!" shouted a boy with red hair.

Then he ran right to the cake table and picked out a chocolate one for his prize.

"Yum!" I said. "This looks like the most delicious game I ever saw!"

I gave the cake lady my ticket.

"Guess what?" I said. "This is my last chance to win a prize. Except for I won a comb. And also I got to throw a sponge at a kid I hate. Plus I jumped till sweat came on my head. But then I couldn't find my shoe named leather. And so that's how come I have a sock foot."

The lady looked funny at me. "Yes, well, uh, good luck to you," she said.

"Good luck to you, too," I said back.

Then I skipped very fast to the squares with the numbers on them.

"OKAY! READY ANYTIME YOU ARE!" I yelled.

But the cake lady kept on waiting and waiting for other kids to come.

It took a very long time. That's how come I got ants in my pants.

I did huffing and puffing.

Then I folded my arms.

And I tapped my foot very fast.

"HEY, I'M NOT GETTING ANY YOUNGER OVER HERE," I shouted.

Finally, the cake lady clapped her hands.

"Boys and girls. I'm going to start the music now. And I would like you to march in an orderly circle. But remember, as soon as the music stops, you stop too."

After that, she turned the music way loud.

I did my bestest marching. My feet were very bouncing. And my knees went way high in the air.

Then all of a sudden—just like before— the music stopped. And all the children stopped, too.

The cake lady reached into her hat.

"Number three!" she hollered out.

I looked down at my square.

"HEY! IT'S ME! IT'S ME! LOOK! I'M STANDING ON THE NUMBER THREE! AND SO I'M THE WINNER, I THINK!"

Mother clapped her hands.

"It *is* you! You *are* the winner!" she yelled.

She had relief on her face.

"Go pick out a cake! Any cake you want!" she said.

I zoomed to the cake table and looked at all the yummy flavors.

There was chocolate. And orange. And lemon. And white. And coconutty. And cupcakes. And doughnuts. And brownies.

Also, there was a secret cake wrapped in shiny aluminum foil!

"What kind is that one?" I asked.

The cake lady wrinkled her nose. "Oh, I don't think you want that one. That one is a fruitcake," she said.

I smiled real big.

"Yea!" I hollered. "Yea for the delicious fruitcake! 'Cause fruit is the bestest thing I love. And so that's the one I pick!"

Mother shook her head. "No, Junie B. It's not the kind of fruit you think it is. You're not going to like it."

I stopped smiling.

"Yeah, only that is not fair and square of you. 'Cause you said I could pick any cake I wanted. And now I pick the fruitcake. And you say I can't have it."

Mother rolled her eyes up at the ceiling.

"Fine. Take the fruitcake," she grouched.

She lifted it off the table for me.

"NO! ME! ME! I WANT TO CARRY IT!" I hollered.

"It's very heavy," said Mother.

"Yeah, only that's how come I have muscley muscles in my arms," I explained.

I bended my arm to show her. "See? See my muscle bump? That's how strong I am."

Finally, Mother put the cake in my arms.

It dropped on the floor.

"Whoa!" I said. "That is the strongest fruit I ever felt!"

"*Now* do you want me to carry it?" Mother asked.

"No," I said. "'Cause I just got a great idea in my head!"

Then I put my heavy cake of fruit down on the floor.

And I dragged it right out of Room Nine!

8/ The Most Usefulest Cake I Love

I dragged my fruitcake down the hall. Mother walked behind me. Her cheeks were very sucked into her head.

"Want to drag it? Want to drag my cake of fruit?" I asked her.

Mother said the word *I'll pass*.

That's how come I dragged my fruitcake to the Moon Walk Tent. All by myself.

And guess what?

Daddy was waiting with my other shoe! It had gotten stuck under that big tent.

And we didn't even see it there!

I put it on my foot. "Hurray!" I said. "Now everything is happily ever after. 'Cause I have my shoes named pat-and-leather. And also I have a delicious cake of fruit! See it, Daddy? See the cake I won!"

Daddy looked at my cake in shiny aluminum.

Then he looked at Mother.

He shook his head very slow. "No," he said. "Don't tell me."

Mother rocked back and forth on her feet.

"Yupper," she said.

Daddy closed his eyes. "You mean she picked…"

"A fruitcake," said Mother.

I jumped way high in the air again. "Yea! Yea! A fruitcake! I picked a fruitcake! And now I would like to see what it looks like.

Only I can't even lift this big guy off the
ground."

Daddy picked it up and set it on the
table.

I pulled off the aluminum foil.

Then I just stared and stared at that
thing.

It was brownish and slickish. And there
was slippery shine on the top.

"It got rotted," I said very quiet.

Mother smiled a little bit. "It's not rotten, Junie B.," she said. "That's just the way fruitcakes look."

I looked closer at it. "Yeah, only I don't even see any fruits on this gunky thing."

Daddy pinched off a little piece for me to look at. He showed me some hard green things. And some hard yellow things. And some hard red things. He said those were the fruits.

I put my tongue on a green one.

"Yuck!" I said. "Bluck!"

Just then I heard a voice.

"JUNIE B.! JUNIE B.! LOOK WHAT I WON AT THE CAKE WALK!"

I turned around.

It was my bestest friend, Lucille. She was running at me with a box of fluffy white cupcakes. They had beautiful rainbow sprinkles on them.

"See them, Junie B.? See how delicious they look?" said Lucille.

"Yeah? So?" I said.

Lucille looked on the table where my cake was.

"What's that?" she asked. "Did you win a cake, too? Can I see it, please?"

I jumped in front of it.

"No. You cannot," I said.

Only Lucille stood on her tippy-toes. And she peeked right around my shoulder.

She made a sick face. "Ick," she said. "What happened to it?"

"Nothing happened to it, that's what," I said back.

I quick put the aluminum foil on it again.

Then I climbed up on the table bench. And I pumped up my muscles. And I lifted my fruitcake way high in the air.

"This could kill you if I dropped it on

your head, Lucille," I said very straining.

Lucille ran to her nanna speedy quick.

After that, I got down from the bench. And I dragged my cake of fruit all the way to my car.

Daddy unlocked the door for me.

"Get in. And I'll set your fruitcake on your lap," he told me.

"Yeah, only that thing will squish my legs into flatties," I said.

And so Daddy put my fruitcake on the seat beside me.

I climbed on top of it and buckled up my seat belt.

"Hey. I can see out the window when I sit on this thing. And it doesn't even smush down," I said.

Daddy made a rhyme. "Fruitcake. The *seat* you can *eat*," he said.

"Yeah, only I never even want to taste

this yucky blucky thing again," I told him.

Mother smiled. "But that's the great thing about fruitcake, Junie B.," she said. "You never actually have to eat it. Because it never goes bad."

"Fruitcake has been known to last for years," said Daddy. "And if you ever get tired of it, you just put a bow on it. And you give it to someone you hate for Christmas."

Then him and Mother laughed and laughed. Only I didn't even get that joke.

Pretty soon, Daddy drove the car into our driveway.

I carried my fruitcake into the house.

Except for just then, it started to slip out of my arms. And so I quick plopped it in my kitchen chair.

I climbed on top of it again.

"Hey! Look how big I am! I'm all the way raised up to the table. And this

fruitcake doesn't even hurt my behiney!"

I smiled very happy.

"This is the most usefulest cake I ever heard of!" I said.

After that, Daddy carried my fruitcake into my room for me.

He put it on my shelf.

Then him and Mother tucked me into bed.

I waited for their feet to walk away.

Then I took my flashlight from under my pillow. And I shined it on my fruitcake.

The aluminum foil sparkled in the dark. It was the most beautiful sight I ever saw.

I smiled some more.

'Cause I am a lucky duck to win that special thing.

And also, I appreciate my comb.

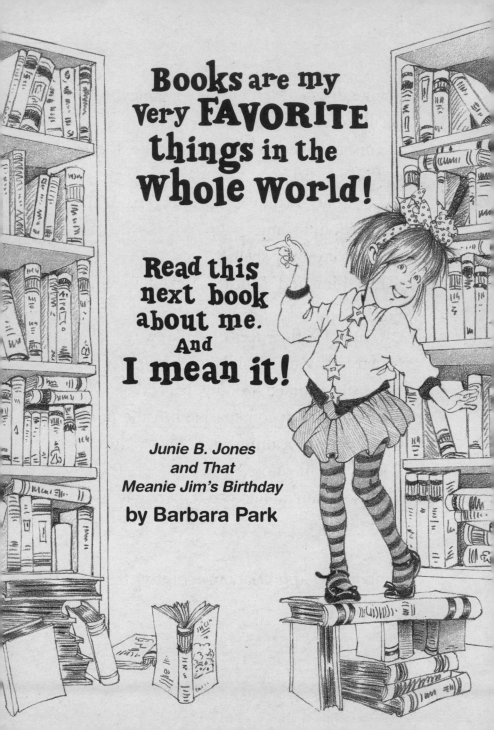

Books are my very **FAVORITE** things in the **Whole World!**

Read this next book about me. And **I mean it!**

Junie B. Jones and That Meanie Jim's Birthday

by **Barbara Park**

I picked up the telephone. Grampa Miller made his voice real quiet.

"You haven't even heard the best part yet," he whispered. "Guess what I'm going to be fixing?"

"What?" I asked.

"If your grandma hears, then *she'll* want to be my helper, instead of you. Ready?"

"Ready," I said.

"Okay. I'm going to be fixing the upstairs *toilet.*"

Just then my mouth came all the way open. 'Cause fixing the upstairs toilet is a dream come true, that's why!

From *Junie B. Jones and That Meanie Jim's Birthday*

Barbara Park says:

66 For some reason, our family always had bad luck at school carnivals. The year my son David won the Cake Walk, there was only one cake left and it tasted like cardboard. The next year, someone stole my son Steve's new shoes while he was leaping around inside the Moon Walk Tent.

Little did I know that all of these disasters would come in handy when Junie B. Jones went to her own school carnival. In fact, with a little imagination, I found I could make Junie B.'s carnival experience even worse than our own!

Or at least I tried.

Leave it to Junie B. Jones to find the bright side of a fruitcake! 99